# Season Tickets

# Season Tickets

*stories and poems by*

## Dan Gilmore

Pima Press

TUCSON, ARIZONA

Published in the United States of America by:

Pima Press
c/o Meg Files, Chair
Department of English
Pima Community College West Campus
2202 West Anklam Road
Tucson AZ 85709-0170

mfiles@pimacc.pima.edu

First Edition

Names, characters, places, and incidents, unless otherwise specifically noted, either are the product of the author's imagination or are used fictitiously.

The author and publisher wish to acknowledge the publications in which the following poems and stories previously appeared: "A Note from Nashville," *Atlanta Review;* "Season Tickets," *Aethlon;* "The Student," "Gravity," "My Father's Toolbox," *OASIS Journal 2002;* "Okies," "The Student," "Seabreeze," "Afraid of Death," "Small Town Boy's Liberation," "Group Shower," "Immortality," *SandScript;* "My Father's Toolbox," "An Evening with My Ex-wife," "At the Annual Friends of the Library Sale," "Group Shower," "Small Town Boy's Liberation," *Loft and Range.*

Cover Design: Leila Joiner
Cover Photograph: Allison Sligh
Book Design: Leila Joiner
Edited by: Tom Speer and Nancy Wall

ISBN 1-931638-01-2

See page 99 for other books published by Pima Press.

 PimaCommunityCollege

*for JoAn, Jennifer-Grae, and Danny*

*Teachers of my heart*

# contents

*part one*

# OKIES

A gust of hot wind blew sand and bits of broken weeds into the boy's face. He cupped his hands around his eyes and watched his father dig, sensing but not understanding the anger that propelled each shovelful of rock and sand to the mound at the side of the grave. "Five years I've been digging graves for others," his father had told the boss man. "I guess I'll dig hers too."

The boy noticed the way his father grunted with each shovelful, how he rolled his head when he paused to wipe his brow, the way his eyes slipped off things instead of looking at them. "Promise me you'll not grow up to be like your father," his mother had said. Now he watched and tried to understand what it was he was not supposed to be.

Several small stones rolled back into the hole. The boy moved to block them with his foot, then stopped. He didn't want to look into the grave. In the corner of his eye, shadows flickered over the sand. He squinted into the sky. Two hawks at opposite sides of a circle turned on waves of heat and disappeared behind the scrub hill in the distance.

"Okie Ridge," one of the miners had said after church, raising his voice as the boy and his mother passed. "Nothing but poor white trash."

"Think they'll get hired on at the mine," another miner said. "They'll get hired, all right, soon as we run out of niggers and drunk injuns."

"Arizona Okies is even dumber than California Okies," the first man said. "Too dumb to make it to California. That's why we got stuck with 'em."

The boy's mother tightened her grip on his hand as they walked away from the church and up the dirt road. The boy had to trot to keep up. "Why'd those men say those things about Okies?" he asked.

She squeezed his hand tighter. "Hurt," she said. "Some people figure they can make their hurt less by giving it to others." She stopped and wheeled the boy around to face her, her green eyes fixed on his. "From now on we ain't missing one damn church meeting even if we have to crawl on our bellies to get there. And every time we go, we're going to look those miners in the eye and smile like we had a feather up our butts. You hear me?"

"Yes'um," the boy said, frowning to keep from smiling.

"Damn right," she said. She threw her head back and let out a whoop. The sunlight behind her made the ends of her red hair glisten like polished glass. "Let's show these people how proud-Okies walk," she said, squaring her shoulders and looping his arm through hers. "Just like the King and Queen of England, the damn King and Queen."

From the cemetery the boy could see the tarpaper shacks with tin roofs that lined the hill like bad teeth. His was the smallest one, just down from the Pattersons'. "Rats," his mother had said when they moved in. "This place ain't nothing but a damn breeding hole for rats." The Pattersons' place was larger and had an icebox in the kitchen. Mr. Patterson got hired on at the mine a year ago. "More education than your father," the boy's mother explained. "Patterson got through the grades."

To the north two smoke stacks boiled out tunnels of sluggish white powder that settled and kept the valley dust-white. The boy had gotten used to his eyes stinging and the sour taste at the back of his tongue. "It's the mine that killed your mother," his father told him. "Sure as if they'd held a gun to her head."

"I can't pay you no two dollars for digging your own wife's grave," the bossman had said. "Best I can do is take a dollar off the cost of her box and marker."

The boy looked at her wood marker. It rested against another one at the next grave. "What's her marker say?" he asked. His father didn't answer.

Clumps of dirt hung in the air, then fell onto the mound. What would it be like for the baby still inside her? When had it died? Could it still be alive? Suddenly a large bone came up out of the grave and landed at his feet. The boy flinched but held his ground. "That some person?" he asked, controlling his voice.

"Cow leg," his father said, hoisting a large rock to the edge of the hole.

The boy flipped the bone with his toe and remembered when that old orange cat first came around, how his mother put chicken bones out for him. "Never know when a cat might come in handy," she said.

A dust devil blew his mother's marker over and, from underneath, a horned toad skittered toward her grave. The boy righted the marker and traced the letters with his finger. "What does it say?" he asked again.

His father tossed another shovelful and pulled himself up. He lifted a leg over the edge and lay on his stomach before standing and brushing the dust from his overalls, dust so fine it hung in the air around him. "Says you ask too many questions." He paused and looked at the sky. "Mrs. Patterson took care of that. Ask her. She's the one that reads."

The boy waved away a fly buzzing around his ear and looked back at the marker. He had not known his father couldn't read. "I can read the letters," he said. "It's just the words."

Last winter his mother taught him how to write his name. "It's time we got you in school," she said. "You're already two grades behind. When your brother's born, you'll have to teach him things." The boy stood beside her, his hand on her stomach, trying to feel the baby move. Suddenly she rocked forward and made a straight line with her finger on the frosted window pane. She attached a curved line to the bottom and a short, straight one at the top, then rocked back, tilted her head, and looked at what she'd done.

"That's a J," she said, "the first letter of your name. Now you make one."

The boy's hand shook as he made a J of his own. How could something as important as the first letter of his name be made with two straight lines and a curved one? "J," he said, "for John," and a smile broke across his face.

"Damn right," she said.

The next morning she taught him the second letter. Each day he learned a new letter. Then one morning while he was eating oatmeal, the letters came together in his head. He went to the window and printed his whole name—JOHN EVERT GORDON. And as he made the marks, something came alive inside him. He took possession of his name; it became a part of him as surely as the air he breathed and the food he ate. It was a gift so large that all his Christmases and birthdays together couldn't match it. He felt enlarged by it, as though his body could barely contain it.

"I'm so proud of you," she said.

"It just came to me," he said.

Her smile vanished. "John, I want to tell you something. Most everything changes. People die, even stones wear away over time, but your father is one who don't change." She thumped the boy's head with the tip of her finger. "He can't think for himself. If somebody ain't around to push him in the right direction, he'll keep going until he falls off the edge of the earth. Promise me you'll not grow up to be like your father."

"I promise," he said, looking down at his hand, the one that knew how to write his name.

It was the boy's first funeral. Mr. Patterson and the two miners who'd said those things about Okies after church helped his father lower the wood box into the hole. When one of the men looked up at him, the boy remembered what his mother had said about feathers. He squared his shoulders and smiled as big as he could. The man's face turned red and he muttered something the boy couldn't hear.

The box knocked against the sides and settled unevenly on a large stone. The sound of the falling stones hitting the top of her box made the boy's knees weak. Why are dead people buried so deep? What if you need to dig them up? He reached for Mrs. Patterson's hand. She was bone-thin, the tallest woman he'd ever seen. Her gray hair hung limp on her shoulders. She held her crying baby in one arm. "Poor thing ain't strong enough to raise another child," his mother had said, "much less a sickly one." Mrs. Patterson's boys stood stiff between her and Mr. Patterson. One elbowed the other and they bit their lips to keep from laughing. Mr. Patterson gave them the eye.

The fat woman who led the choir at church sang "Amazing Grace," and when she was nearly finished, Mr. Patterson spat a stream of tobacco juice onto the mound of sand. It hung there, then rolled down, collecting dust as it went. The boy was relieved when it stopped short of the grave. No one else seemed to pay it any mind.

The boy's father stood alone on the other side of the grave arranging sand with his toe. He wore the same shoes he'd dug the grave in—hightops, flat at the heel and white with dust. The sole of his right shoe had come loose, and his laces were undone. "If I wasn't around, neither one of you would remember to tie your shoes," his mother had said. "You're the image of your father." The boy checked his shoes. He had remembered.

The sun was fierce, and the preacher talked like he didn't have enough spit. "Would you bow your heads, please," he said.

The boy watched his father, one hand resting on the shovel handle, the other clenched tight at his side. The preacher finished his prayer: "Lord, their hearts are still, and they are at peace in heaven."

Mrs. Patterson's hand had turned wet and cold. Her baby was crying.

"We say goodbye now to this good woman and her guiltless child," the preacher continued. "The Bible says offer the sacrifices of righteousness and put your trust in the Lord. That is what Sister Gordon has done. May she rest in peace."

The woman sang "In the Garden" as people drifted away, shaking hands and calling each other brother this and sister that. Mr. Patterson shook hands with the boy and his father. "The wife will cook some for y'all," he said. Then he walked back to the hill with his sons.

Mrs. Patterson stayed behind. While the boy's father filled the grave, she stood next to the boy and nursed her baby. The boy was listening to the baby's sucking sounds when the horned toad he'd seen that morning shimmied out of the sand and made a run for it. His father stabbed at it with his shovel and cut the toad in half. The two pieces twitched and tried to pull apart but were held together by a fine string of flesh.

Without thinking, the boy wrapped his arms around Mrs. Patterson's legs, almost causing her to lose her balance. "My Lord, be careful, Mr. Gordon," she said.

The boy's father's eyes narrowed. "Just whose Lord you talking about, Mrs. Patterson?" He scooped up the toad and tossed it aside.

Mrs. Patterson lowered herself to her knees and put her arm around him. He could smell her clean wet breast. The baby started crying again. Mrs. Patterson adjusted her dress and held the baby to her.

"Hand me that marker o'er there," the boy's father said.

The boy avoided his father's eyes as he carried the marker back toward the grave. When he passed Mrs. Patterson, he held it up and whispered, "What does it say?"

She touched the words with her long fingers. "Hattie Belle Gordon—Beloved Wife and Mother—1922-1947." Mrs. Patterson closed her eyes. "Bless her heart," she said. "She was only seventeen when she had you."

"Hattie Belle," the boy repeated. He handed the marker to his father. "I never knew she had a name."

The summer days got hotter and drier. The motionless air buzzed with the sting of heat. The tarpaper on the outside of the house smelled, the oilcloth that lined the ceiling sagged. The boy sensed it was best to keep his distance from his father, but with only two rooms, it wasn't easy. His father avoided the bedroom except to sleep. He spent most of his time sharpening his pocket knife with a whetstone while sitting on the front porch or at the small metal kitchen table with flaps—flaps no longer used. The boy sat across the room on his sleeping mat pretending he was different from his father. Neither he nor his father would sit in his mother's rocking chair. The boy was afraid to look at his father and afraid not to. They had tried to talk, then his father had gone stone silent. "A mad dog is most dangerous when he ain't barking," his mother had told him.

One evening the boy sat cross-legged next to the rocking chair pretending to read an old newspaper. Outside thousands of crickets trilled in the hot night air. From up the hill the Patterson baby cried; it seemed never to stop crying. At the metal table his father cut chunks of the cornbread Mrs. Patterson had made. He stabbed a piece with his pocket knife and dipped it into a bowl of pinto beans; his teeth clicked together. He washed the cornbread down with gulps of water and made muffled wet sounds.

The boy turned the pages slowly, as she had done, and tried to see her fingers as they separated and lifted each page up and across to the other side. He pretended he could read the words as she had read them to him. He heard her voice forming the sounds, her labored breathing, the sudden coughing that jarred his head as it rested on her breast.

His father drank the juice from the beans. It dripped from the corners of his mouth onto his undershirt. He was drenched in sweat and the boy could smell him from across the room. A cricket sounded a high-pitched chirp. It was under the table. His father picked up one of his shoes and crushed it. He hit it a second time, picked it up, and stared at it. His eyes rolled up and he made a sound as if he were sinking deeper into a dark hole.

Something inside the boy tightened. "Do you want to learn to write your name?" he asked. "I can help you."

His father looked straight ahead at some great sadness the boy could almost see.

A short time before she died, the boy's mother had nudged him awake in the middle of the night. "Shh," she said. "You know where that orange cat is?"

"Under the porch, I guess. He sleeps under there now."

"Find him and put him in your pillow case. Tie a knot in it so he won't get out, and wait for me outside."

The boy found the cat and slipped his pillow case over him. The cat was too sleepy to put up much of a fight.

His mother stood on the path holding an empty gunnysack and motioning for the boy to follow her.

He hoisted the cat over his shoulder. "Where we going?" he whispered.

"Shh. Over to old man Jeffries' to borrow some chickens."

"Ain't that stealing?"

"Lord no. Stealing is in the heart. This is just borrowing. We'll pay him back with even bigger ones as soon as your father gets on at the mine."

"Why we taking the cat?"

"To give old Jeffries something to shoot at besides us in case he hears us. Hurry before your father wakes up."

"Maybe he could help."

"Maybe the moon is made of mashed potatoes."

In a flurry of feathers and squawking chickens, they got three roosters but lost the cat. It had almost cleared the fence when Mr. Jeffries blew half its head off.

The next morning the boy's mother wrung the chickens' necks, dipped them in boiling water, and plucked them. "Too bad that cat ain't around to eat the innards," she said.

Later that afternoon the boy saw the cat hanging spread-eagle on old man Jeffries' fence. Jeffries had slit him down the middle, and his insides were hanging out. The boy wanted to run but made himself stay. He inched closer until he could see the cat's one glazed eye. He could smell the shiny lumps of blood, hear the flies buzzing as they swarmed on strings of rotting flesh.

He found a broken tree limb, lifted the cat's heavy innards back into the cavity of its body, and pushed the flaps closed. The bailing wire around the front paws came untwisted easily. The cat, still spread-eagle, thumped face down into the sand. The boy sucked in a breath and forced himself to look at the cat until the fear left him.

"Why'd old man Jeffries do that?" he asked his mother.

"To scare off any other cats that might have the same idea."

"The cat didn't have the idea. It was your idea. He was sleeping."

"But old man Jeffries didn't know that. Things die sometimes so other things can live. The Bible calls it righteous sacrifice. That's what these chickens did. That's what the cat did. He made a righteous sacrifice so we could live." She rolled the pieces of chicken in seasoned flour and dropped them into sizzling lard. "I'll skin you alive if you tell your father how we got these chickens. You hear me?"

"You ever wring a chicken's neck?" Mrs. Patterson asked. She was holding two chickens by their feet.

"I watched my mother," the boy said.

"It's time you learned."

The boy took a chicken from her and pressed it against his side. He could feel its wings pushing out against his arm and ribs. Its head bobbed back and forth as though it were pecking gnats from the air. He cupped his free hand around the chicken's head and tightened his grip. All he had to do was let go, but he paused and his arm wouldn't move. "I don't want to," he said.

Mrs. Patterson smiled. "You'll do it when it's time." She took the chicken's head in her hand, looped it around twice, and the headless chicken hit the ground running. She repeated the motion with a second one. She and the boy stood together watching the headless chickens run around the yard.

"Why don't they run into each other?" the boy asked.

Mrs. Patterson shook her head. "I ain't never thought about that," she said. "Maybe you should ask your Pa."

"You think I should bury those heads?" the boy asked.

Mrs. Patterson picked up the two chickens. "Yes," she said. "You go bury them."

Later in her kitchen the boy watched her cut up the chickens, roll the pieces in flour, and drop them into the hot lard. They both jumped back and laughed. At that moment he wanted more than anything to live with the Pattersons, and the shame of wanting it made him miss his mother all the more.

～

On her bad days she'd cough, spit up blood, and stay in bed, but on good days she'd let the boy help her mop, bake bread, pick through the beans for bad ones, help with the laundry on the washboard. One morning after they'd hung the clothes on the line, she bathed and asked him to help her wash her back and hair. He piled her soapy hair on top of her head and slipped the lye soap over the freckles on her shoulders.

"Can you count them?" she asked.

"About a million," he said.

She rinsed her hair with a mixture of water and vinegar. "Walk into town with me," she said.

They bought some onions and potatoes at the mercantile, then went store to store looking for old newspapers and magazines. "You have to learn about the world," she said. "One piece of paper is as good as another when you're starting on empty."

That evening at sunset they sat on the front steps and she read to him, a story about the first Negro baseball player, another about a woman preacher who claimed to heal people through prayer and laying on of hands.

"Does prayer really make things better?" the boy asked.

"I damn sure hope it does," she said. They sat in silence for a moment.

"That's the prettiest sunset I ever saw," the boy said.

"Go tell your father to stop sharpening that knife of his and come sit with us."

The three of them sat on the steps. When it was too dark to read, she told stories, one about picking cotton, another about how she met the boy's father. "If your father hadn't married me, I was fixing to propose to the neighbor's mule," she said. "Had to get out of that dust bowl. Didn't figure I'd end up in a worse one." She slid her hand up his father's back and scratched his head. The boy had never seen her touch his father that way before.

His father grunted and rolled his head in a circle. "You'll be gettin' out soon," he said. "Better air in California."

"But we had some fun," she said. "I remember once how me and sister pretended to be wild animals and built a nest out of leaves and twigs under the house. Mama thought it was a possum and came crawling in after us with a broom handle." She laughed and put her other arm around the boy. They sat in silence for awhile, looking into the milky sky.

His father rested his hand on his mother's upper leg. "Real nice night," he said.

When she tucked the boy in that night, she held back a cough with a blood-stained rag she'd started carrying with her. Her lips were dry and rough on his; her breath smelled old and thick. He went to sleep thinking about the three of them sitting together and talking, their legs almost touching.

The next morning Mrs. Patterson shook him awake. "You come home with me," she said.

The boy dressed by the wood stove where he could see his mother. The mesquite tree outside the bedroom window cast a lace shadow over her face and red night shirt. His father sat on the far edge of the bed dipping a rag into a water pan. He slowly folded it and used it to push back ringlets of hair stuck to her forehead. Her eyes were closed, but her mouth open as though she'd stopped in the middle of saying something important.

The edge of summer softened into fall. The sun moved lower. The days grew cooler and shorter. "It's time to register John for school," Mrs. Patterson told his father, but the time came and went.

Tall men in white shirts knocked on the screen door and asked for the rent. The boy's father shrugged and gave them what he had. "This'll have to do," he said.

"You ain't making enough to stay here," Mrs. Patterson said.

"I ain't making enough to leave either," he said.

Then one day the boy heard the sound of a siren coming from the direction of the mine. It went on and off all afternoon. That evening he and his father stood on the porch and watched Mr. Patterson come up the path.

"Oh, thank God. You're alive," Mrs. Patterson cried.

"How bad was it?" the boy's father asked.

"Bad," Mr. Patterson said. "They're hiring. Need men to help dig out the dead. Better hightail it down there."

The boy watched from the shack as his father made his way down the road. He wondered if his father would make enough money to have his floppy sole fixed. His father didn't come home. Two more days passed. He came home coated in gray mud.

"The boss man said I could outdig three Mexicans," his father said.

With his first check, he bought a sack of flour, a bushel of potatoes, and a slab of bacon. One of the widows offered them an old icebox for ten dollars, and he bought that too.

While his father worked, the boy sometimes crawled under the porch and watched the thin slices of sunlight inch across his body. Or he might climb to the top of the hill where he could see her grave. He could no longer remember her face, the sound of her voice when she read to him, the feel of her hands. At home he'd wash his hands in lye soap, rinse them in vinegar and water, cup them and hold them to his nose.

When Mrs. Patterson's baby had convulsions and died, the boy's father dug its grave, the smallest grave the boy had ever seen. In the days after the funeral the boy helped Mrs. Patterson while her boys were in school. He folded laundry, swept and mopped the floor, washed dishes. She fed him dinner and sometimes supper, and when his father worked nights, he'd sometimes sneak back, stand outside the Pattersons' bedroom, and peek through their window.

One night he watched Mrs. Patterson standing at the end of the bed brushing her hair. Mr. Patterson lay in bed, the covers drawn up to his neck.

"The Gordon boy wants to come live with us," she said.

"He asked?"

She sat on the edge of the bed. "No, but I can tell it's what he wants."

He took her hand. "It ain't possible."

"I know," she sighed. "I know." She rubbed her hands up across her ribs and over her breasts. "I hurt from not nursing," she said.

Mr. Patterson raised to one elbow. "Let me see."

She unbuttoned her nightshirt, pulled it open, and lay beside him.

Mr. Patterson put his mouth first to one breast, then the other. Mrs. Patterson began to sob. Mr. Patterson hugged and kissed her. The next morning the boy went through the cardboard box where Mrs. Patterson had packed his mother's clothes. He found her red nightshirt, took it to his place under the porch, and stayed there all day holding the soft smell of her against his cheek. It was dark when he heard his father's footsteps. He folded the nightshirt and left it under the porch.

That evening the boy sat in the far corner eating a boiled potato. His father sat at the kitchen table, eating fried round steak and drinking iced tea. He ate like a stray dog who had been invited into a stranger's house. His eyes darted from the stove to the ceiling to the kitchen sink, as though he was looking for a place to escape. He took out his pocket knife and began to sharpen it.

The boy wondered if his father was going mad. He wanted his father to look at him, to say something. He missed his mother more than ever. He wanted to hear her stories, have her read to him. He tried to remember the sound of her laughter that night before she died. He looked up and saw something move, a bulge in the oilcloth lining the ceiling. Had his father seen it? He waited. It moved again.

"Rat," he whispered.

"Huh?" his father said.

"Rat," he repeated. He pointed. "There in the ceiling."

"I don't see—"

"There's a sag in the oilcloth. It's moving."

They waited. There was a faint high-pitched squeak. The oilcloth moved again.

"There, see it?" the boy whispered. "How'd it get up there?"

"Looking for a place to nest maybe."

They fell silent and listened to the small, busy squeaks.

The boy's father stood and held his open knife above his head.

The boy came to his feet. He felt as though he was floating. His knees shook as his father slid across the floor and stopped under the sag. It moved. His father moved the knife with it, waited. Then just as the rat paused, he plunged the blade through the oilcloth. The point grated against the tin roof. The air seemed to leave the room, then the rat screeched, a sound exactly like a baby crying. His throat knotted. His father's arm stiffened as he held the knife rigid. The rat fought, grew silent, then fought again.

"Hold on, hold on," the boy whispered, twisting his body in sympathy with the rat's movements.

Slowly the dance ended—a spasm, another smaller one, then silence. Sweat covered his father's face. He pulled the knife back through the oilcloth. Blood collected at the hole. He cut it larger. A gray rat slipped through the rupture and tumbled to the floor. Tiny pieces of straw and shredded newspaper floated down behind.

"Nesting," his father said. "Fixing to have babies." He nudged her with his foot. "Throw her in the bushes out back."

The boy stood over the rat. A drop of blood stuck to the corner of her mouth. He picked her up by the tail and carried her toward the door. The tail felt smooth and warm in one direction, rough in the other. She weighed more than he expected. He was almost to the door when the rat gave a violent jerk. Her teeth were chattering. He dropped her and jumped back.

"Throw her out, I said."

"She ain't dead."

"Then kill her." He slid his knife across the floor.

The boy stared at the knife, then the rat.

"Go on," his father said.

He picked up the knife, got on all fours, and held the tip of the blade several inches above where he thought the heart was. A white wind rushed through his head and he pushed the blade through the rat.

"That's it," his father said. "Good."

He stabbed a second and third time. The rat lay in a pool of blood.

"You got her," his father said. "I'll be damned. You got her. I thought you were afraid."

"She needs to be buried," the boy said.

Outside, he crawled under the porch, scooped out a hole and buried the rat. He held his mother's nightshirt for a while, then buried it too. When he went back inside, his father was sitting in the rocking chair. The boy picked up the knife, wiped the blade on his pants, and closed it. "Here," he said, handing the knife to his father.

"My name is Frank," his father said. "Frank Ernest Gordon. Couldn't write it if my life depended on it."

The boy tried to repeat his father's name but couldn't get it out.

"I have an extra dollar or two. It's yours. What can I get you?"

The boy cleared his throat and sat down at the kitchen table, hands folded. "A knife of my own," he said.

## MY FATHER'S TOOLBOX

I was past being impressed by anything
an adult could do when he talked
me into going to the dump. I kicked
at a stiff work glove, threw a couple
of stones at some gulls, and said
I'd wait in the car. He held up
a rusted pair of pliers and a drill bit
and said he couldn't believe anyone
would throw something like this
away. I said I couldn't believe
he could say something that dumb.
At home, he put the pliers and bit
in a box he'd made of scrap wood—squeaky
hinges, edges worn smooth over the years
by hands rough as files. Nothing useful inside—
a screwdriver with half a handle,
a hammer stained with tar, baby food
jars filled with bent nails, rusted screws,
tangled string. I asked what he planned
to do with all this junk. He shrugged, closed
the box, gave it a pat, and said I'd missed
the point. When he died a few years later,
I threw the toolbox away. I'm alone now,
the same age he was when he died,
and I'm sitting in my back yard
like an old dog who stays put
long after his fence has fallen.
There's a rusted gate that's lost
its swing, a ladder no longer safe
for climbing, a patch of weeds
grown large as women's

legs, and I'm thinking of my father,
wondering when it was he came to understand
how we cling for all we're worth
to that sweet wreckage we call our lives.

# GROUP SHOWER

Cold, naked boys huddle together
without touching, pale hands
clasped at their groins, shivering,
listening attentively as the teacher
displays a jock strap on the end
of a stick and tells them about
the horrors of jock itch.

Water and steam engulf them,
but they are still cold. Their lanky
blue bodies ascend like statues
through a fog-blanketed lake
on a moonless night, and in this
watery stillness a sweet naïveté
freezes them, makes them

impenetrable. Here, each boy is born
into a secret brotherhood of fear.
Each will spend his life inventing
and reinventing himself, polishing
the surface of himself, never sure
what's his and what's theirs,
wondering why he's so cold,
and why, no matter which direction
he turns, he can't get close enough
to the fire.

# SMALL TOWN BOY'S LIBERATION

Sunday is his day. He owns the town.
He doesn't bother peeking in library
windows or checking the Texaco
to see if the bathroom's locked—
that's weekday after-school stuff—
but goes straight to the post office,
pushes open the brass door, breathes
the emptiness, turns the wire wastebasket over,
climbs on top, and stands nose to nose
with the *Most Wanted.*

No trouble choosing—
eight men with killer ears
and slanted eyes, and a couple
of women to cook. He jumps down,
kicks over the wastebasket, yells
*This way men,* and runs. He leaps
the hedge and darts down the alley.
He calls the dog chasing him a *shitfucker,*
clears the fence, plows through roses,
crushes snapdragons, dives into weeds
behind his garage, and eyes the enemy—
his father in his undershirt mowing
the shitfucking lawn, his mother
on the porch reading her Bible.
He crawls closer and whispers,
*Stay low men and keep the women quiet.*

# HEARTBREAK HOTEL

Bald, barely five seven, obese,
with pudgy arms and dull, wet
eyes, my father was more pug
dog than human. At least I believed

that the day I stuck a tattered
Elvis wig on his head, shoved
my old guitar into his hands,
turned up the volume and urged

him to mouth the words, strum
the guitar, and shake his hips.
Somehow I believed if he'd do
only this, it would be proof

he loved me, that he would
play catch with me, take me
camping. But he stood frozen
in the middle of the room.

I wanted to kick him, to make
him scream in pain. Then just
before the record ended, his eyes
welled with tears as if he'd caught

a glimpse of someone he loved
in a crowd. I snapped a picture
of that expression, and in the flash,
his eyes clouded over and his smile

vanished. He took off the wig,
and sat for a long time rubbing
the hair between his fingers.
Thirty years later I still don't know

what he was thinking. I'm looking
at that picture now, that expression,
and think of the monkey in the Psych 101
movie, how he suddenly saw

the connection between his stick
and an unreachable banana,
and I wonder if it's possible that,
in those few seconds, my father

glimpsed the possibilities of himself,
realized he could be someone
different, then sensed his utter aloneness?
I think of us, the father and son who shared

nothing, alone under the stars, our tiny
campfire lighting such a small piece of darkness.

# THE MAIN EVENT

My father and I sat on the fenders
of his old Pontiac parked in front
of the department store, drank grape Nehi,
and waited for the main event to start
on the TV set in the store window.
He had lost his job that afternoon,
and my mother's words still burned
my ears—*useless, stupid, helpless.*
I hated him for just standing there,
taking what she dished out, and swore
I'd never be like him. Cheers

as the flying Garabaldis, a father
and son team, entered the ring. Boos
as Red Barry twinkle-toed across
the mat in shoes so liquid red
he must have walked through blood
to get there. More boos for Gorgeous
George, his orchid robe and lavender
curls. I was rooting for George
and Barry. I liked it when, from nowhere,
Barry forearmed the older Garabaldi
and body-slammed him to the canvas.
I cheered out loud when Gorgeous
George delivered a knee-drop
to the throat of the fallen Garabaldi
and he lay motionless, blood flowing
from his mouth. The match was over

before it began, and while the crowd
was still booing my father leapt

from his fender and stood before me,
feet spread, arms flexed like two fleshy
parentheses. "Hit me," he said,
"hard as you can." I stared at my feet.
He moved closer. "I said, hit me. Goddamnit,
hit me." I hit him, all right, drove
my fist into his stomach with all
the power of my fourteen years.
It didn't faze him. I hit him again
and again, until it hurt to lift
my arms. But all he did was jack-up
his pants, swagger back to his fender,
and say, "Shit, that the best you got?"

Mr. Moto entered the ring with his
razor-edged derby and his sidekick,
Tojo. My father polished off his Nehi,
belched and pointed to the screen
with his empty bottle. "I could lick
both those Japs," he said, "that queer
Gorgeous George, too. I could lick
anybody on this stinking earth." I stared
at the screen and forced back tears.
A feeling as soothing as the breath
of God washed over me. I believed
him. Brother, I believed he could.

## MISS MILLER

She invited the whole third grade,
but I was the only one who attended,
proof I loved her most. I giggled start
to finish and broke into laughter the second
the minister said, *You may kiss the bride.*

Monday, carrying a mirrored bowl
from Harmon's, gift-wrapped and tied
with red ribbon made twisty with a skin-tingling
swipe of Mrs. Harmon's scissors,
I hurried past the swings and monkey bars
toward her room, wild to demonstrate my love,
to reassure her nothing had changed. Took

the steps two at a time, ran down the hall,
slid around the polished tile corner, and stood
frozen outside her door, feeling small
and insignificant, embarrassed about
the twisted ribbon and stupid bowl.
What difference could I make in her life now
that she had abandoned me? My heart turned cold,
and I buried the bowl in soft soil under a bush
behind the backstop. That was fifty-six years ago.

She had four children before her divorce.
The youngest went to Stanford. The oldest
played baseball at UCLA and spent some time
in the majors. Still looking for that smile
and nod of approval, I saw her briefly on a recent
visit back. She's in her nineties now, almost
blind. I paid my respects and asked about

her health, afraid to ask what I really
wanted to know. She took my hand
but didn't remember me. I don't know

what happened to her bowl, but choose
to believe it's still there under that bush,
filled with the part of me I buried with it.

# CHRISTMAS '51

Willowy Aunt Bell, boasting
a 197 scratch average, received
a bowling ball from my father,
a ball like no other, clear plastic
with a real lily embedded inside.
My father told her the ball

was like her, hard on the outside,
beautiful inside. Later, I sat on it
outside the bathroom, peeked
through the keyhole, and watched
my father masturbate. Jerry Glover
had told me you did it while thinking

about a vagina. I'd never seen
a vagina, but Jerry said imagine two
Twinkies placed side by side.
So I sat on the ball imagining
those Twinkies while *Oh Come
All Ye Faithful* played on the Philco,

but all I got was hungry and curious
about whose vagina my father
was thinking about, as scents
of roasted turkey and sage dressing
drifted down the hall with my mother's
cooking sounds and Aunt Bell's laughter.

She told my mother she'd never seen
a clear-plastic bowling ball before,
and how sweet of my father.

He closed his eyes, raised his head
to the nozzle, and pumped faster.
Aunt Bell said she'd bet there

wasn't a prettier ball in all of Grayson
County, and wasn't it amazing
how far down into that flower
you could see. I looked between
my legs, down into the lily. Goose
bumps covered my arms. I knelt
before the ball, opened my pants,
and joined my father, thinking
of that lily, oh so dark inside,
*Oh Little Town of Bethlehem*,
the words, the music, those rogue
smells, and Aunt Bell's laughter.

*Above thy deep and dreamless*
*sleep, the silent stars go by.* My father
spurted a white rope into the tub.
Seconds later, I did the same, amazed
at the blurry smoothness of my own
semen hovering over the lips of the lily

on Aunt Bell's bowling ball. My father
cupped his hands, took three tiny steps
and released an imaginary ball. I could
almost hear pins scatter. In the kitchen
Aunt Bell laughed and said wasn't it good
that I was interested in bowling, since

an interest in anything by a boy my age
was rare. O*h, Holy Night* played as I cleaned
her ball with a sock, then took it to her and asked
if she'd take me bowling sometime. My father
walked in smiling. She pushed at her hair.
Of course, hon. Maybe your father can come too.

# FIRST TV

My mother took a moral stand against it,
said television was the work of the devil,
said my father's wanting it showed how
weak he really was. But, for once, he stood
firm. It was a blond GE with a twelve-inch
screen—a blond whore my mother couldn't
have hated more. After supper, we sat on the sofa

in the dark, my mother wedged in the middle,
hands over her ears, back straight, her worn,
leather Bible on her lap. My father switched it on.
Roller Derby came at us like a train on fire,
women on skates trying to kill one another—
knees to the midsection, elbows to the neck,
hair-pulling, eye-gouging. Suddenly my mother

leaned forward and yelled, "Kill her. Oh, kill her.
Hit her in the mouth." She jabbed us with her elbows,
moved to the edge of the sofa. Her Bible lay splayed
at her feet like an injured player. During a commercial
she read aloud from John 12:46. *I am come a light
into the world, that whosoever believeth on me
should not abide in darkness.* Amen, she said as the men

took the track. She marked her place with a finger,
sat forward again and yelled, "Kill him, kick him.
That's it. Oh, hurt him." My father excused himself
to get a glass of water. I sat on the floor to escape
her sharp elbow. And, years later, this is the way
I remember her: alone, agitated, the empty space

around her expanding, the wild, festering pleasure
she took in wrestling, boxing, and roller derby, that Bible
always within reach, proof to all that a better place awaited her.

# MUD BABY

At seventeen I hitchhiked cross-country,
looking for my parents. Stopped at revival
meetings for free food, at carnivals
and fairs for a day's work, thinking
they might do the same. One night

in Iowa, a storm hit. I crawled under
a truck, watched fingers of rain turn
dust into mud, and thought of the time
my father and I played in a bog, how he
called me his mud baby and tossed
me into the air. I remembered

that feeling just before he let go,
how I held on so tight I could feel
both our hearts beating, how I
wanted that wild anticipation
to last forever. Found them a year

later, running a three dollar
flophouse in San Bernardino.
Both beat up pretty good. We
hugged but didn't pretend
anything. She said they
thought I'd do better on my own.
He said he'd heard farmers
were hiring pickers in Sacramento.

Gave me a free room to rest up,
but the bed smelled of piss
and the guy next door vomited

all night. I left before sunrise,
happy I'd caught up with them,
happier to be set free.

*part two*

# THE STUDENT

Sunday, 11:52 p.m. Wendell Sears sits cross-legged in the middle of his bed in his so-called room at the back of the wedding chapel. He holds a Benzedrex nose inhaler in one hand and his statistics book in the other. For an hour a fly has been banging up against his greasy window. He can't understand why the stupid thing doesn't just give up. Wendell is about to. He opens the inhaler and sniffs. It makes his eyes water.

"It'll increase your IQ by twenty points," Max said.

Max has a straight A average, has a way with women, can impersonate almost anyone. Max says the secret to his success is Benzedrex inhalers. He eats four a week.

In his bathroom Wendell cracks open the plastic tube, removes the cotton core and the little piece of paper with the skull and crossbones, and washes the whole thing down with a glass of water. "Don't forget the little piece of paper," Max warned. "It has the good stuff."

12:58 a.m. Since taking the nose inhaler Wendell has performed two more weddings. He doesn't feel any smarter; his penis is half its normal size, and he's burping great clouds of menthol. He does another wedding and tries to study again, but the two sides of his heart are racing like greyhounds. The ratty air-conditioning units at LaRue's Motor Lodge next door sound like a hundred cats in heat. It feels as if tiny ants are crawling across the surface of his brain. He isolates one and follows it from his cerebellum up to his temporal lobe and into his Fissure of Rolando. His powers of concentration are amazing. The inhaler is working. It's time to get serious. He picks up the phone and dials Norwood's number.

"Lo," Norwood says in that blubbery nasal tone of his, half yawning.

"It's me. Wendell. I've been studying statistics. Thought you might be able to help me."

"Shit, Slim. I don't know squat about statistics."

"I got a test tomorrow. Need to close the chapel for a few hours."

"Staying open is how we pay the bills, Slim. Ain't my fault you don't know shit about self-discipline. Move 'em in, move 'em out. Stop taking yourself so goddamn serious."

"If I flunk I won't graduate."

"What's statistics got to do with anything? Your talent is in ministering, Slim. You're a people person."

Wendell prepares himself for Norwood's future of America speech.

"The future of America is weddings and funerals, Slim. More people are getting married and dying than ever before, and that number jumps up like a goosed heifer every year. Stick with me, we'll both be sucking some playmate's tit in the back of our own Lear jets. You with me or not, Slim?"

"I'm with you, Norwood," Wendell says.

Wendell drinks another glass of water and opens his book, but he can't stop thinking about three-hundred-pound Norwood sucking a playmate's tit. The image sort of disgusts him. On the other hand, he appreciates Norwood recognizing his potential as a people person. He's right, though, about Wendell's lack of self-discipline, but bombing through a ceremony isn't Wendell's style. Every wedding is an opportunity to participate in a sacred event, a pivotal moment that changes the course of people's lives. And he's good at it, better than any regular minister who does one or two a month and uses a canned ceremony. Wendell performs sixty to seventy weddings a week, and he does his best to make every one of them unique and meaningful. He composes his ceremonies, gives people what they want—a sign of the cross for Catholics, a reference to karma for Hindus, even some down-home Bible-thumping for Baptists. He never judges. Once he symbolically used a riding crop on an S-and-M couple pretend-ing reluctance. Another time he put on war paint for a couple who were into an American Indian thing. Just last week he wore high heels and a wig to perform a wedding for a cross-dressing couple. Norwood is right. People are Wendell's thing. Performing weddings is about the only thing he does that makes him feel good about himself.

He opens his book again.

The fly crashing into his window is driving him crazy. He rolls up a magazine, takes a wild swing at the fly and misses. He looks everywhere, but the fly has vanished. He sits up and reads aloud about something called hypothesis testing.

*Truth can never be arrived at with one hundred percent confidence, only approximated through testing the null hypothesis. The null hypothesis is based on the assumption that the world is a booming, buzzing confusion of unrelated elements colliding randomly with each other. Scientists, on the other hand, assume randomness and attempt to demonstrate orderliness among these elements by rejecting the null hypothesis.*

Okay, he sort of understands this. His life, for example, has been a mixture of confusion and chaos, while Max's is disciplined and predictable. Most days Wendell spends dodging one disaster after another, grasping at straws, wandering up dead-end streets. Max always has goals, a plan, an answer for every problem.

The phone rings.

Wendell's mouth is dry. He can barely speak. "Norwood?"

"Is this the Chapel of the Bells?" The woman's voice is almost childlike.

Goose bumps cover Wendell's arms. He clears his throat and lowers the pitch of his voice. "Yes, this is Reverend Sears."

The woman explains that she and her fiancé are from California. She wants to know if the chapel is open all night.

"Do you have your license?" he asks.

"We got it this afternoon," she says. "We're just not sure we want to get married. You see, we—"

He knows from past experience this conversation is about to go on for an hour. "I'm sorry," he says. "There's someone at the door." Then he adds, "Look, I'll be here all night if you decide you want to go through with it." He hangs up, feeling bad he cut her off.

*The sum of the deviations from the mean squared should not be confused with the sum of the squared deviations from the mean. Both are crucial in computing the standard deviation.*

It has something to do with figuring out what normal is. All his life Wendell has been trying for normal, but keeps slipping to the downside of the bell curve. Max calls it the domino effect. One screw-up leads to another screw-up, Max says. Max lives his life on the opposite end of the bell curve, several deviations above the mean. "Think shit, be shit," he says. "Think success, be success."

2:15 a.m. The doorbell rings. It's a couple of drunks with no license. Wendell doesn't tell them the Carson City office is open all night. They shouldn't be driving. Instead, he gives them one of Norwood's business cards and tells them they can get ten percent off on the bridal suite next door at LaRue's.

Ten minutes later he dials Max's room number at LaRue's to see if the couple showed up. They didn't.

"How's the studying going?" Max asks.

"Did the inhaler," Wendell says, "but people keep coming."

"Hey, Twila," Max calls, "Wendell did an inhaler."

"Cool," a woman's voice says.

"Who's Twila?"

"Dancer at the Nugget. Wants to play drums in my new band."

"What about the menthol?" Wendell says. "Can't stop burping."

"Don't worry about it," Max says. "Takes a week or so to go away. Sweetens your breath."

"I was just wondering if maybe you—you and Twila—could watch the lobby for awhile, greet people, do the paper work. I gotta study."

A brief silence. Then, "I'm sorry, buddy. It's just that Twila and me—Look, I haven't told anyone yet, but I'm thinking of moving to Vegas, starting an Elvis band. Twila's going to be my agent and drummer."

"Oh," Wendell says.

"I'm tired of doing Lash LaRue," Max says. "What's the point impersonating someone no one ever heard of?"

"I've been doing that my whole life," Wendell says.

"Look, buddy. This friend of Twila's is coming over after she's off work. Topless dancer at the Turf Club. Horny. Wants to check out our act. Interested?"

"I gotta study."

"Hey, maybe you could play backup guitar, be a stand-in Elvis on my night off."

Wendell doesn't tell Max he's tone deaf, and for a second he imagines himself on stage singing "Love Me Tender," which to him is the saddest song Elvis ever sang. "I'll give it some thought," Wendell says.

"Think of it this way. There are two hundred thirty-seven Elvises in Vegas, and every one of them goes to bed at night knowing who he is. You can be one of them."

2:30 a.m. Wendell has been thinking about what Max said. He likes the part about going to bed knowing who he is.

He opens his book and looks for something he understands, but he can't help thinking about the topless dancer. Maybe he should say hello to her, but truth be known, he has trouble relating to women who expose their breasts to perfect strangers. He can't help thinking all that gawking would suck the life right out of them. He hasn't met the right woman yet, but he is certain she won't be a topless dancer.

2:33 a.m. He carries his statistics book to the lobby and sits at Norwood's big mahogany desk. No, he decides, he won't learn to play guitar and be a substitute Elvis impersonator. Impersonating Elvis is Max's thing. Wendell's dream is to set up a counseling practice in a small town like Winnemucca or Elko, maybe work with depressed hookers or retired blackjack dealers. He wants to get married someday, join the Rotary and Elks, maybe coach Little League, stuff like that. If he flunks, he'll have to work for Norwood the rest of his life. Not that the money isn't good. In five years Norwood has gone from a K-Mart baby photographer to just short of a millionaire, but there's a sleaziness about Norwood that bothers Wendell. Norwood has started collecting art and expensive wine, for example, but still lives in a doublewide.

41

*We assume anything can be measured, and what can't be measured doesn't exist or isn't significant.*

Wendell can go along with this. Even love can be measured if you think of it as not just a feeling but a set of actions. Even his performance as a minister can be measured. According to Norwood, the tear-to-ceremony ratio—a statistic that Norwood follows closely—is the key indicator of success. By the end of the first semester, Wendell had increased his tear ratio from one cry in ten weddings to eight in ten. Norwood claims tears yield a forty-percent higher gross. Wendell doesn't care about that, but nothing matches the feeling that comes when the bride and groom tear up. If he has trouble drawing tears, he makes a video of himself and tries to spot what he's doing wrong. Almost always the problem is the pacing. "You want tears, you have to learn the art of the pregnant pause," Norwood says. For all his faults, Norwood has it right when it comes to tears. He isn't the worst boss a person can have.

2:37 a.m. Wendell looks around the room at the red satin drapes, the display of rings, the plastic corsages that cost Norwood about ten cents to make, his statistics book.

*The coefficient of correlation when squared can be interpreted as the amount of variability in variable-A that can be accounted for by the variability in variable-B.*

All the little V's look like tiny hinges flying across the page. He stares at this paragraph and, in a moment of clarity, has an intuitive, goose-pimply understanding of how almost everything in the universe is connected to everything else and how something that isn't connected is somehow—*in error.* Suddenly, he feels sad and doesn't know why.

2:45 a.m. He is bug-eyed, dry-mouth panicked and getting higher by the minute. The doorbell rings. His heart almost stops. "Just a minute," he calls. He walks around in a circle a couple of times, hurries to his bedroom, tosses his statistics book on his bed, bangs on his sternum to regulate his breathing, clips on his tie, slips into his baby-blue blazer, and answers the door.

"Hi," the girl says. He recognizes the soft, childlike voice. "We've decided to tie the knot."

They are three or four years younger than Wendell. Her eyes are rimmed in red as if she has been crying. Bad mascara, thin upper lip, full lower lip. The boy's expression is somewhere between Where-am-I? and I-think-I'm-going-to-be-sick.

"I'm Reverend Sears," Wendell says. "Come in."

They step inside and stand for a minute, staring at the wall filled with Norwood's plastic corsages.

"Permanent mementos," Wendell says. Statistical terms and formulas are flying around like bats in his head. He skips asking the boy if he might be interested in buying a corsage for his new bride.

The boy sits stiff-backed in a chair, holding a copy of *Gray's Anatomy*. His unblinking eyes remind Wendell of the rabbit he hit while driving a couple to Carson City in Norwood's limo. It seems important to mention the rabbit. "You know," he says, "last week I ran over a rabbit on my way to Carson City."

"Oh, I'm sorry," the girl says.

"I hadn't given it much thought, but in a way it was a miracle. I mean, think about the forces that conspired to make me and that rabbit end up in exactly the same spot at exactly the same time."

The girl nods.

"What if I had been driving a tenth of a mile an hour slower or faster? What if the rabbit had stopped to scratch behind its ear? There we were, the rabbit and me living our lives—hopping around, driving a car—and suddenly, *Bam*, the rabbit ceased to exist. Does this feel like an accident to you?"

The girl looks at Wendell. "Yeah, that's right, you know. I mean everything's like that. We just keep bumping into one another."

"I know," Wendell says. She has understood what he's getting at.

The girl walks around looking at everything. "Nice," she says, paging through Norwood's display of wedding photos and videos. She studies the rack of rings, the brochure about tuxedo rentals, the sample wedding book. She's wearing one of those full dresses with a velveteen top. Her skirt rises up in front because she's pregnant. Six or seven months, Wendell guesses. Big eyes, short dark hair, pretty in that pale Northern California way. She carries a little white sequined purse that sparkles when the lights catch it. The purse seems out of place.

"Nice purse," Wendell says. "Something borrowed?"

"Yes," she says. "My mother's. She insisted."

"Mothers," Wendell says.

"Yeah," the girl says.

Wendell sits at Norwood's desk. "May I see your license?"

The boy digs through the pockets of his stringy cutoffs and hands Wendell a wadded-up, coffee-stained license. Their names are Richard Holt and Jane Fisher.

Wendell almost laughs. "Dick and Jane?" he says.

Jane smiles. "We know."

"Richard," the boy says. He's wearing a Stanford University T-shirt. Wendell points to his anatomy book. "Have you matriculated at Stanford?" he asks, striking a balance between formal and friendly. His palms are suddenly sweaty.

"I'm a junior at The Farm," Richard says. He holds up his anatomy book. "Premed. My father's a radiologist." He laughs nervously. "Old blood and guts, they call him."

Wendell notices Richard has one blue and one brown eye and finds it difficult to look directly at him. He focuses on Richard's forehead, and lies. "I applied to Stanford, but Nevada Reno offered me a larger scholarship."

As he fills out the license, he thinks about the improbability of Wendell Sears, a hick from Globe, Arizona, ending up a minister in a wedding chapel with a girl named Jane and a guy named Dick with different-colored eyes. The idea staggers him.

Jane is humming and fiddling with the plastic flowers. She is a good person, Wendell decides—curious, alive, a good listener—but he wonders about her choice of mates. Maybe Richard represents the security she needs. One of the problems with the wedding business is that he'll never see them again, never know if Dick and Jane are a good match. Still, he wants her to have a good experience. He'll take his time and give her his best. "How about you, Jane? Do you go to Stanford?"

"I graduated from Stanislaus Community College," she says, "honors."

"And how did the two of you meet?"

"In this cocktail lounge in Palo Alto where I work," Jane says, "a place called The Hutch. Have you heard of it?"

"Name sounds familiar."

There's a long silence. Jane sniffs one of the plastic flowers, then turns to Richard. "We're okay with this, aren't we?"

Wendell burps and fans it away.

Richard's body contorts as if executing a simultaneous shrug and grimace. "Sure," he says. "Aren't you?"

Wendell tells them he has to call some people to serve as witnesses, that it will be five or ten minutes. In his bedroom he dials Max's number. Max is in the middle of "Blue Suede Shoes." He says he and Twila will be over as soon as they work out the coda.

"What's a coda?" Wendell asks.

"A big ending," Max says.

Instead of using the time to hustle auxiliary sales—photographs, plastic corsages, audio or video recordings, rings, tuxes, wedding gowns—Wendell lights the candles, turns on The Thousand Strings rendition of "Because," and goes to his room to lie down for a few minutes. Maybe his ceremonies need a coda, he thinks, something unforgettable, an amazing insight. He can't keep the thought going. His heart has positioned itself about two feet in front of him and is pulling him along like he's on a leash. He's clammy all over. He bites his lip to keep from throwing up.

3:12 a.m. Max and Twila arrive. Dick still has his nose in his anatomy book.

Jane stares at Max, who is in his all-white Elvis outfit. "Very cool," she says.

Max does a hitch with his hips. "Mighty fine meetin' ya, hon," he says in perfect Elvis. He introduces Twila all around as his agent and drummer.

"Jeez," Jane says, wide-eyed, smiling. "A real Elvis."

Now there are five of them in the same room, six counting Jane's baby, all from different places, here for different reasons, to accomplish one thing—the marriage of Dick and Jane. A chill crosses Wendell's shoulders. Does this mean anything or is it all just booming, buzzing confusion?

"This way," Wendell says.

He lines the four of them up and taps the foot control under the carpet to lower the volume of "Because." The candles glow brighter than usual. He takes a breath, manufactures a moment, and begins. "We are gathered here in the presence of Max and Twila to proclaim and celebrate the love of Dick and Jane."

"Richard," Dick whispers.

"Sorry." Wendell continues, interweaving themes of probability and love and how chaos and our interpretation of it has contributed to a sense of the divine. He doesn't understand everything he's saying, but Jane seems to. This one's for you, Jane, he thinks, entrusting the details of his ceremony to the muse. As he speaks, a part of him leaves his body and floats up to the ceiling. This higher part of himself observes Wendell the minister from a distance, admiring how his brain leaps along ahead of him, gazelle-like, planning every inflection, marking every pause. Wendell winks at Jane.

She smiles. Her eyes are sparkling, her delight obvious.

Richard looks confused, but what does a radiologist's son know?

Wendell raises his oratory to a higher level. "Who's to say how these two beings from Palo Alto and San Jose found each other at a bar called The Hutch? The mystery of how we come together in this life is one of the great mysteries of—this life. The important thing is, we mysteriously come together."

Another perfect pause.

"What we know, my friends, is that love is present in this room, that the Null hypothesis has been rejected." He looks directly at Jane and she looks back at him, obviously on the verge of tears. "We can taste it in the air, feel it in our breath, hear it in the music."

Jane is caught in the headlights of Wendell's oratory. He has her. The dam will break when they exchange rings.

"And tonight we celebrate this palpable mystery of love, this perfect love, with the perfect symbol—the never-ending, continuous, perfect circle of the wedding bands." At this moment it dawns on Wendell that he has forgotten to ask if they have rings. He holds out his hand, hoping.

"We don't have rings," Richard says.

Jane shudders and blinks. "Hurry," she mouths.

Wendell's mind locks up. It's as though the film has broken in a movie and Wendell is staring at a blank screen. The mood is destroyed. His tear ratio is in the toilet. There's a squirmy silence.

"Borrow rings from the rack in the waiting room," Max says.

Max is amazing.

"Wait here," Wendell says. "Don't move." He returns with two rings, confidence restored, more determined than ever to get tears.

"Jane, place this symbol of your love on Richard's finger, and repeat after me. 'With this ring on thy finger, I thee wed.'"

It goes perfectly. Jane looks on the verge of a major catharsis.

Wendell turns to Dick. "Richard, place this symbol of your eternal love on Jane's finger and repeat after me. 'With this ring…'" Just as Richard slips the ring on Jane's finger, her knees buckle. She drops to the floor.

A faint, Wendell thinks. Incredible. You get a faint once every two hundred weddings. He can't wait to tell Norwood.

Jane's head jerks back, her spine arches, she starts writhing around. Wendell recognizes the symptoms. He's seen them before, a girl in his abnormal psych class. Jane's having an epileptic seizure. He kneels over her for a few seconds, then looks up at Max. He'll know what to do.

"Ohmygod," Twila says, the back of her hand to her mouth.

"Epileptic fit," Max says, as if naming it takes care of everything.

Richard stands in the shadows at the rear of the chapel, palms flat against the wall as if he's glued there.

Max hasn't moved. He looks out of place in his Elvis outfit.

"I'll get a pillow. Elevate her head," Wendell says.

"Shouldn't she bite on something?" Max asks.

"Old wives' tale," Wendell says. "Get a cool wash rag for her face." He turns to Richard who has slid down the wall and is in a sitting position without a chair. "Has this happened before?"

Richard shakes his head. "She never told me anything about fits." He looks around, every place except at Jane. "I have a test. Excuse me, I—" He stands up and tucks his book under his arm. "I can't do this. I don't even know her. My parents would kill me." He lunges toward the door. A few seconds later, Wendell hears the squeal of tires.

Jane is still convulsing, but less so.

"I gotta get back to LaRue's," Max says. "Twila and I—"

"Sure," Wendell says. "Go."

3:23 a.m. Jane is sleeping now. Wendell folds his jacket and places it over her. He stays close, not wanting her to wake up and have no one to look at. "Because" keeps playing. A couple of candles flicker and go out. He wipes some spittle from the corners of Jane's mouth and pushes her hair back from her eyes.

3:35 a.m. She opens her eyes and looks around.

"You're going to be fine," he says.

"Where's Richard?"

*Run Dick run*, Wendell almost says. He nods in the direction of the lobby.

"Are we married?"

"Not yet." He feels bad for her. "Should you go to the hospital?"

"I'll be fine," she insists. "I'll get help if there are complications. Don't worry. I've been through this before." She seems in control, clear about what she wants. She closes her eyes again and sleeps.

Wendell wishes Max had stayed.

"Because" plays through twice more. Wendell strokes Jane's cheek lightly with his finger and she wakes up. She can't remember anything they talked about.

"Where's Richard?"

"Gone."

"Oh."

"Would you like to spend the night in my room? There's only about three hours of it left. You can figure out what to do in the morning."

She licks her lips. "Thanks."

Wendell turns off the music, snuffs out the few remaining candles, switches off the neon sign, and locks the door. He'll deal with Norwood's wrath later. He tries to help Jane to her feet, but she's wobbly and starts to go down. He catches her, holds her in his arms, carries her to his bed, and accidentally puts her down on his statistics book.

Jane straightens her skirt and crosses her ankles.

Wendell feels dizzy. His upper lip twitches. "I think I'm about to faint."

She pats the bed. "Lie down beside me."

He takes off his tie and shoes and lies beside her. He notices the metallic smell of her breath, how her dress rustles when she turns to face him. "There's something hard under me," she says.

He feels under her and removes his book. "Statistics. I have a test at nine this morning."

They lie side by side, facing one another. Her eyes are still goofy-looking, but dry.

"I'm sorry," Wendell says. He burps a quiet one.

"You smell good."

"You too."

"Your eyes are so—intense."

"Do you want to talk about Richard?"

"What's your first name?"

"Wendell."

"Wendell," she repeats.

"Jane."

"Give me your hand." She places it at the side of her stomach and holds it there. Something moves. Wendell jerks back.

"The baby's awake," she says.

"I've got to rest," Wendell says.

"Close your eyes, Wendell."

He closes them, but they pop open. "Can't."

49

She's already sleeping. He spends the rest of the night burping menthol and looking at her face. It's the most amazing face he has ever seen.

6:58 a.m. The fly returns. It lands on the back of Wendell's hand. He looks at it for awhile. It seems calmer. He shoos it away, and nudges Jane awake.

"Do you have a toothbrush I can borrow?" she asks.

He watches while she brushes her teeth. He has never loaned anyone his toothbrush before. It seems so—intimate.

7:23 a.m. He takes Jane to the A&W down the street for a Mama Burger and coffee. He has coffee and watches her eat, suspecting that any minute she'll realize what a mess her life is, and the tears will start to flow.

"This is the best food I've ever eaten," she says.

He nods. "Are you okay?"

She tells him about Richard, what a good student he is, how his family was against them getting married. "I think I got pregnant the first night he took me home," she says. "We hardly knew each other. He tried to talk me into getting an abortion, but I didn't want one." She pauses to sip her coffee. "Now he's gone."

"Gone," Wendell says.

"Bastard," she says.

"Shithead," Wendell says.

She finishes her burger, wipes her mouth, and asks, "What denomination are you?"

He doesn't want to say Nevada Mission Fellowship. "Lutheran."

"I'm not anything," she says. "I meant to tell Richard about my seizures but kept putting it off. I have a new medication, haven't had a seizure for over a year."

"I don't think of the ministry as a vocation," Wendell says. "I've been trying to graduate from college for eight years. It's my senior year, and I'm about to flunk out." He feels his throat tighten. "I guess I'm a little scared."

"What's your major?"

"Counseling."

"And you're taking statistics?"

"Uh huh. Required. If I flunk, I don't know what I'll do."

She touches the back of his hand and sucks in a breath. "You won't flunk. Trust me. You are very smart."

"Really?" Wendell takes some comfort in this because he remembers reading somewhere that epileptics possess certain powers after their seizures.

8:08 a.m. At the bus station he buys Jane a one-way ticket to San Jose. They sit on a bench, side by side, facing opposite directions, her the bus yard, him the front door.

"Each of us facing our futures," she says. "Just us rabbits hopping around." She reaches for his hand.

"Yeah," he says. "You going back to The Hutch?"

"Probably." She takes a pen from her purse and writes her phone number on the back of his hand. "Call if you're ever down my way."

Wendell can't speak.

8:15 a.m. Before boarding her bus, she squints into the sun, shields her eyes with that little purse of hers, and says, "Thanks for spending my wedding night with me."

"You're welcome," he manages.

She boards and waves from the bus window.

He waves back until the bus pulls away.

8:28 a.m. He drives up Virginia Avenue trying to decide if he'll take his exam or go back to the chapel. Norwood will be there, mad as hell, but Wendell knows how to handle Norwood. In the gambling district the neon signs are still on, but the sunlight is sapping the magic out of them. Tired-looking people who have been gambling all night are leaving the casinos, crossing paths with fresh ones, people with renewed hope, eager to get an early start—all the sure-fire systems gone bust meeting the hopes of a new day.

The sun reflects off his hood. He stops for a light at Fourth Avenue and tries to read a line or two from his book, but he can't help thinking of Jane sitting on the bus, heading back to her life in San Jose, The Hutch, that little purse in her lap, how she refused to cave in, how Richard and Max ran away. As he pulls away from the intersection, he feels a swelling in his chest, a physical understanding that at this moment everything is in its place doing what it's supposed to be doing, one moment giving birth to the next in an endless chain of small miracles. He turns onto Campus Avenue and finds a parking place right away. That in itself is pretty amazing.

## INDEPENDENCE DAY

I awake and realize
we've slept in separate beds.
It's 100 degrees already.
The swamp cooler motor
screeches its angry protest
against heat and overwork.

You're in the kitchen trying
to be quiet. I hear the scrape
of a skillet, smell burnt toast.
I lie motionless, thinking
of the dry undergrowth
of love, its brittle hate,
how a match carelessly tossed
can destroy it. As I enter

you look up, tell me
fireworks are banned
this year, too dry.
Firearms too, you say.

# QUITTING

When the quality of Yokohama Rice Bowl's
teriyaki chicken began to seriously deteriorate,
you told me you couldn't understand why
I persisted filling out my Buy-Ten-Get-One-Free card.
I told you, I'm not a quitter. By my eighth bowl,
the rice was gummy and the chicken smelled moldy,
but I kept going back and finally ate enough
to order my free bowl. It was even moldier
than the rest and, as I finished it, some heroic
quitters I've known came to mind—a Tucson
man who spent two thousand on a drum set,
then walked away because he hated practicing.
Another who charged a new Harley on his Visa,
found a brave woman, took off cross-country,
and made it as far as Vegas before he decided
to leave her. A dear friend who, in the space of a year,
became a failed novelist, a not-quite-certified
swimming instructor, a former sculptor,
a born again Christian, and an atheist.
I admired their lack of tenacity, their ability
to walk away. On the whole they seemed happier
than me. But a beaver cannot become a swan.
I called you on my cell phone and told you
I'd just finished my free bowl. How was it?
you asked. Lousy, I said, but it'll be better
next time. You're crazy, you said. Don't leave,
I said. Then I waited a full minute, listening
to the dial tone, before hanging up.

# A NOTE FROM NASHVILLE

On Highway 40 just west of Nashville
a sign caught my eye: *Garden of Eden, Five Miles,*
and I couldn't help wondering why Adam and Eve
would want to share Paradise with a total stranger.
Was this their real punishment—banishment to Paradise,
forced for all eternity to pick hibiscus and eat
persimmons? After all, how long can anyone cling
to Paradise before it becomes tedious? I guessed
it was Eve's idea. I imagined her, after forty million
years, still flush from discovering another kind of flower
and fed up with Adam's snoring, poking him awake
and saying, *You must paint a sign.* Chances were,
at this moment, she was there at the entrance, her body
lush in dappled sunlight, giving nervous little touches
to her hair, as she awaited her first customer.
Would it be me? I'll admit I was tempted. Then another
two miles and I imagined Adam, brow furrowed, perplexed
that persimmons no longer tasted the same, and I had a hunch
he preferred the simple pleasures of occasionally
peeking out at Paradise, then retreating back to more
familiar slugs and mosses. It occurred to me that, like Adam,
I have difficulty appreciating abundance while you
thrive on it. That's why I love the sparseness of the desert,
the occasional wild flower sprouting in the midst of nothingness.
So when the next sign said *Turn here,* I thought of you
bedded down with your new lover, happy again, and I kept
my foot on the pedal, turned on the radio, and headed
for the city of sad music, loyal dogs, and lonely hearts.

# EMPATHY INTERRUPTED

I trace the rim of my glass
with an attentive finger. Two hours
we've been talking about ex-spouses
and how much we miss our children.
Now she's telling me about a floor lamp
her ex-old man stole from her and how
he ruined it painting the shade
with black enamel. I am discerning
innuendo here, detecting nuance, but lose
my concentration because in the next booth
a man and woman are arguing about ferrets.
He's saying he'll replace her goddamn ferrets
but won't pay the vet's bill. She's crying
and saying she doesn't want his replacement ferrets,
she wants her original ones. He reminds her
that her original goddamn ferrets are dead,
and she says something about ferrets
not being replaceable like engine parts.
The woman next to me is still talking
about the lampshade, measuring
my compassion over the rim
of her glass. She asks, is she
just imagining it, or is the world
totally fucked? The ferret woman
says fuck you and leaves. I try
not to blink, but those ferrets
are still in my head. I take a sip,
breathe, execute a slow nod, and say,
I know exactly how you're feeling,
and all the while I'm trying
to remember how long it's been

since I've cared for anything
as much as that woman cares
for those ferrets.

## THE MORNING AFTER

Why did I drink it—a full pint of Old Crow
on top of a plate full of fettuccine?
And that motel with the moldy shower curtain.
So cheap.
So disgusting.
And the woman's—God, I can't even remember
her name—her chipped front tooth, her insistence
on saying "me and him."
So sleazy.
So unsophisticated.
How could anyone with sensitivity and conscience
be expected to perform under those conditions?

# AN EVENING WITH MY EX-WIFE

Water pours off her roof
in streams the size of snakes. We sit
at opposite ends of her new sofa,
sip ouzo, and listen to her new
Lena Horne CD, the hiss
of a bad speaker. A second ouzo
and I tell a lie about skydiving
lessons. A third and she tells me
she's met an artist who paints vipers.

An hour has passed. She curls
her legs under her, smoothes
her skirt. Her head moves
to a tune she's humming. I chew
an ice cube and wonder what
it would take to stop her humming.
This artist, I say, which particular
vipers does he paint? Her eyes flare,
then she wags a finger and says
I'd better go.

A block away my car stalls.
Water everywhere. My wipers
just smear things around.
I stand outside and feel the rush
of water around my ankles.
I look for the curb, a fallen branch
to hold on to. I check her house
just as the porch light dims.
I draw a breath, stand motionless,
and hope nothing strikes.

*part three*

**M**yers' right side drags behind him as if it's a dead body part he's trying to shed. He feels as if he could walk right out of the dead part of himself back into his old life if he could get his mind just right, think just the right thoughts. But he can't concentrate, can't tell a right thought from a wrong one, can't even remember his old life.

"No people," he says.

"Now your right leg," Miss Choy says. She walks a step behind him, instructing, urging him on, treating him like a child. "You spend more time with people," she says.

He wills his right leg to move and moves in the direction of the single table at the near corner of the dining hall. No one is sitting there. Maybe the new person has forgotten.

"Lady not here yet. Miss Choy get you settled, then find her."

At the table, he pulls the chair back. He lowers his body into it, loses his balance, and falls the last six inches. His walker bangs to the floor.

The dining room is silent, then the noise resumes.

Miss Choy retrieves his walker and stands at his side, arms folded. "No problem. Open napkin," she says.

He finds the corner of the napkin, holds it between his thumb and forefinger of his left hand and shakes it open.

"Spread on lap."

He manages to place it across his knees.

"You getting better. Miss Choy give you 'A-minus' in napkin today."

The waitress comes, a mere child.

Myers waits for Miss Choy to order for him.

"You make order today," she says.

He sits up straight and speaks slowly, trying to control the spasms of his lips and tongue. "Boiled egg…dry toast…coffee."

He looks up at Miss Choy, pleased that the words he intended were the words that came out.

She gives him a wink.

He uses his napkin to dab at the spittle at the right corner of his mouth, and manages to return it to his lap. The color is a pleasant sea blue, the same color as his bed sheets and the furniture in the lounge. But there's no sea here, no breeze either, just sand and cacti and a cloudless glaring sky, so bright it seems white. Sometimes he sits alone in the garden and imagines he is living inside an egg.

He lifts his right hand onto the table and covers it with his left. Touching his right hand is like touching someone else. His left hand can feel the touch of his right, but his right can't feel itself being touched. He concentrates on his left hand and names its parts—fingers...knuckles...fingernails. He names the salt and pepper shakers, the menu.

Miss Choy leans over him. "Before Miss Choy go, tell her your name."

He hesitates, forces his lips together. "Murphy," he says, certain he's got it this time.

"Myers," she says. "Milton Myers."

He smells cigarettes on her breath and wonders if he ever smoked. "Leave...me...alone," he says.

"Practice," Miss Choy says. "You practice."

Myers holds up his left hand. "Fingers," he says angrily. "Knuckles, fingernails."

"Good," she says. "Now your name."

He frowns and stares straight ahead.

"Say it."

He pushes out his lips. "Can't."

Miss Choy uses his napkin to wipe his mouth. "I go when you tell me name."

He tries again. "Myers," he manages this time.

"Good. Now Miss Choy leave you, go find your new lady friend."

"No," he says, but she ignores him. He closes his eyes and retreats into the cave of himself. He hears slurred S's, the click of false teeth, forks tapping on plates, talk of livers and kidneys, cancers and insulin. He smells perfumes and aftershaves. A purple light surrounds everything, not entirely unpleasant, just strange, probably not real. Yet it could be real. It's possible he can see things others can't see. He knows that certain clouds, while invisible in the lighted sky, can still show their reflections in water. Perhaps he is a scientist of some kind.

He sips his coffee. It dribbles from the right side of his mouth.

A hush travels over the room. Everyone is staring at his mess, wishing he'd stayed in his room. Someone opens the drapes. The light is blinding. His eyes water. He looks around for Miss Choy. She's at the entrance, talking to another woman...tall...one long braid...jewelry that catches the light. Miss Choy points to Myers. Both women wave at him and the braided woman heads his way. A hush follows her as she winds her way through the tables. Her gait is slow, but assured, a hint of grace. Attractive...wrinkled skin. She might have been a model, the wife of a rich person, a lawyer. He takes a book from his jacket pocket—crossword puzzles. He has no idea where he got it. He reads an inscription. "Get well quick, Pop, Love Vic." He tries to remember a man named Vic. He can't. All the puzzles are blank. Purple frost rims each white square.

"Milton Myers?" the woman says. "Lily Bryant. I'm new here. Miss Choy told me you might like company." Her voice is low and resonant, from her chest.

He pokes at his boiled egg with his fork.

She cracks it open with his knife, scoops out both halves and sits down in the chair opposite him. "Salt and pepper?" she asks.

"Fine," he says.

"I'm starving," she says, salting his egg. Her hand moves toward his plate, picks up half a slice of his toast, and returns to her mouth. "I hope I'm not intruding," she says.

His toast disappears into her mouth. He watches the up and down movement of her throat when she swallows, the soft, almost transparent skin at the base of her neck.

She orders oatmeal with brown sugar, raisins, and cream. "Perhaps you can show me around later."

He nabs a thought and forms his words. "Don't…have to… sit…here," he manages. "Others more—"

"Look at me," she says. She dips the tip of her napkin in water, reaches across the table, and wipes the corner of his mouth. "That's better. Why? Don't you find me interesting?" The movement of her hands leaves a trace of silvery light that breaks up and disappears.

"I…find…you—" He can't think of a word, then one comes. "Dazzling," he says. He repeats it. "Dazzling."

"Why, thank you." With her spoon she punctures the skin on her oatmeal and probes inside. She takes a bite and looks at him. "Tell me something about yourself."

He must say something, force himself to carry on a conversation. He holds his spoon and sees the grotesque concave reflection of his face. He looks around the full dining hall. "Stroke…You?"

"My lungs brought me here. I came west for the dry air. I was a dancer at Radio City for many years. Later we traveled. What did you do? I mean, for a living." She moves her arm and the bracelets catch the light. For a moment the room is filled with rainbows.

"Optics," he says.

"You make glasses?"

He nods.

"Are you married?"

He shrugs. "Someone…call me…Pop."

"My husband died of cancer. Sometimes I hear that booming voice of his as clear as I hear my own." She pats her chest. "Then something snaps here, and I realize, all over again, he's gone." She takes a spoonful of oatmeal. "I still dance. It helps me forget."

"You…can't forget. I…can't remember." He looks at his hands.

She puts her spoon down. "Sometimes I get so lonely," she says. "Do you?"

Myers shrugs. Suddenly he is sad. "Must go," he says.

It's dark outside. From his chair in his room Myers follows the row of lights lining the pathways in the flower garden that end at

66

the fountain. The fountain erupts every fifteen minutes. Sometimes the fifteen minutes feels like days, other times only a few seconds. He rubs the back of his numb right hand, pokes a fingernail into it, but he can't feel the pain. If that woman sits with him tomorrow, he will ask her to move. The fountain erupts.

Suddenly it's morning, as if no time has passed. He's eating breakfast—another egg, a piece of toast, another cup of coffee—and Lily is sitting opposite him, reading a newspaper. He can't remember how she got there. She's wearing sand-colored slacks and an orange-tinted silk blouse, sleeves rolled up to her elbows. Her lips are fleshier than he remembered. They are orange too. If he were an artist, he might like to paint a picture of her.

She folds her paper, looks at him and says, "You don't seem very talkative this morning."

"Thinking," he says.

"About what?"

*How nice you look*, he wants to say. "Toast," he says.

She sips water and watches him over the edge of her glass. She leans in. "I have a question. Do you want to be my boyfriend?"

He feels dizzy. He remembers a line from a poem or song about tadpoles dancing in the moonlight, unable to see. His eyes meet hers. "You…mean…sex?"

"If we feel like it."

"I don't…think…I can."

"Then we'll just cuddle," she says.

The next morning she asks again if he'll be her boyfriend. He tells Miss Choy, but she only laughs.

After lunch Lily insists they take a walk in the garden.

"Nap," he says.

"Nonsense," she says.

They inch their way through the garden, he with his walker, Lily with her arm looped through his. She knows the name of every flower there and tries to teach him. A name he can remember from the past is *mallow*.

67

"There are none here," she says. "But they are lovely, aren't they, their papery leaves, so delicate and wild."

He wants to open his mouth and have clever words pour out of him. He wants to make her laugh, to squeeze his arm tighter to his side, but all he can manage is "Tired."

"Let's sit on this bench and pretend we're in the middle of a field of mallows," she says.

They sit near the fountain and watch fingers of water trickling down cement grooves and disappearing into the pool below.

She squeezes his arm and leans closer. "And what's that?" She points to a flower with large yellow petals.

"Pretend mallows," he says.

She laughs. "Yes, aren't they beautiful?" Her right pinkie touches his left one.

He doesn't move his hand away until she begins to cough and can't stop.

He tries to sleep, but the rush of water in the fountain sounds like a thousand birds taking flight, bacon frying, the white static on TV. Suddenly he's angry. This place is nothing but a stage setting, something manufactured, a theater for the dying to play out their deaths. His life has left him. His speech has left him. On their next walk he'll tell Lily he wants to be left alone.

She is wearing a broad-brimmed white hat, stacks of gold bracelets, and a white dress.

He can't stop looking at her. "You are dazzling," he tells her.

"Let's walk." She loops her arm through his. The warmth of her body enters his shoulder.

"Maybe you should find someone else," he says.

"Nonsense," she says. She gives him a peck on his right cheek. He can't feel it.

Days pass, just how many he doesn't know. He and Lily are eating regularly together, walking together. She hasn't mentioned his being her boyfriend again.

Then one evening someone is sitting across from him in the lounge, a grown man with curly black hair. He's wearing a blue suit and red tie. His eyes are too close together. He has five o'clock shadow.

"Pop," the man says. "How you feeling?"

Myers doesn't know this man, and he doesn't particularly like him. "Fine."

"Do you remember my name?"

"Yes," Myers lies.

"That's great. It's Victor, Vic Myers. You're looking—great." There's a long silence. "How's the food?"

"Good."

"Great." Long pause. "I watched the Rams play last night. Lost again." He leans closer. "Don't worry, Pop, things are going okay at your office. Stanley says to tell you not to worry. Vicki's a gem. They could use you, though. Some tough cases coming up." He sits back and takes a breath. "How they treating you?"

"Good." Myers remembers hearing a woman scream, the sound of dishes crashing, pinning a boy on the floor with his knees.

"You're looking great. You're going to be fine."

"Fine," Myers says. He wants this man to leave him alone. He wants to see Lily.

"We're doing well, aren't we," Victor says. "I mean the two of us." He lowers his head. "Maybe there's still time to—"

"Tired," Myers says. "Please go."

That evening Myers and Lily watch TV in the lounge. She places her right hand over his left and holds his hand until the movie ends. He can't concentrate on the movie.

The weather has turned warmer; shadows are getting shorter. Myers wears a summer suit and bow tie. He found a wristwatch in his dresser drawer. "It Rolex," Miss Choy says. "You very big, big shot."

Miss Choy is teaching him how to tell time. The big hand is on the twelve, the small one on the eight. "Twenty to twelve," he says.

"Tell me story about your wife," Miss Choy says.

He has no stories to tell. "Can't," he says.

Lily has stories. She can talk for an hour on any subject. She tells him about her travels in Italy, her favorite restaurants in Manhattan, about meeting an Arabian prince who liked to talk dirty.

"What is your favorite ice cream?" Lily asks.

"Peppermint stick," he says.

"Mine too," she says.

"I have a son," he says. "His name is Victor."

"How wonderful."

"I don't like him," Myers says. "Maybe I've never liked him."

"Nonsense," she says.

They watch a video of *South Pacific* and watch it again the next night. She tries to get him to sing along, pokes him in the ribs. He laughs. The sound of his own laughter surprises him. His heart races.

His thoughts are becoming less chaotic. He can order them, line them up and deal with them one at a time. He saw a spider in the garden and remembered its name—black widow. This morning he looked at a calendar and wondered aloud when he might be leaving this place.

"Maybe when you work crossword puzzle," Miss Choy said.

He works half the night and finishes only a third of it. But his face and hand are regaining some feeling. He uses a cane now instead of a walker.

Lily's coughing is worse. When they walk she has to rest every few minutes. He finds himself becoming slightly impatient with her. One day she shows up with a cane.

"I never thought this would happen to me," she says.

They walk arm in arm, each with a cane. He remembers the names of two flowers—snapdragons, daisies. "I'll pick a rose for you," he says.

"They're all artificial," she says.

"Impossible," he says. "I can smell them." He examines the stem of a rose. A thorn bends and springs back. "Goddamnit," he says.

70

"At our age so much depends on our imaginations," she says.

The thought crosses his mind to tell her he loves her.

She touches a flower with her cane and remains silent for a long time.

"Time to get you back," he says.

Suddenly the shadows have retreated under their objects. Myers stops wearing a tie and leaves his cane in the closet. He remembers being a lawyer, defending a gun manufacturer in several lawsuits. He remembers someone calling him one tough son-of-a-bitch. He can speak in complete sentences.

Lily has hired someone to redecorate her apartment. "Isn't it too bad we can't start over," she says, "discover parts of ourselves we never knew, love more, be outrageous more, do all the things we feared most?"

"Do I get to see your apartment?" he asks.

"Not until it's finished. I'm doing my walls white," Lily says. "White carpet, too. I plan to hang pictures of myself, blown-up poster-sized photos taken of me when I was a dancer. That was the best time in my life." They stop by the fountain. She moves the tips of her fingers back and forth in the water. "You're leaving soon, aren't you?"

"I want to get back to work," he says.

"Were you planning to tell me?"

"I'll take on small cases at first, then we'll see."

"Do you have a photo of yourself?"

He doesn't, but says he'll ask Vic for one.

That night he reads the *Law Review* Victor brought him. He swivels his chair to face his sliding glass door and looks at the rectangle of light beyond the garden, Lily's door. He sniffs his hand, searching for the scent of her perfume.

By late summer Lily is using an oxygen canister. She spends most of her time in her apartment and never turns off her lights. At night Myers sits in his chair looking alternately at Lily's door and the reflection of his head in his own sliding door. He can't remember what he looked like before his stroke. He asked Victor for a picture, but Victor said he burned everything after his mother died.

"How did she die?" Myers asks.

"Sleeping pills and booze," Vic says.

"Oh," Myers says. "Am I to blame?"

"Yes," Vic says.

"Your mother lacked courage," Myers says. "You are very much like her."

Lily uses a walker now. Her shoulders hunch forward. She coughs and strains for breath, her voice almost a whisper. They sit in their usual place near the fountain. Lily plucks her rose, pulls it up by its artificial stem, sniffs it.

"What if everyone did that?" Myers says, taking the rose from her. "There'd be no flowers for anyone to enjoy." He sticks the stem back into the soil.

They sit for a few more minutes.

"May I hold your hand?" she asks.

He lets her. "See how the reds and greens fade into shades of gray as the sun sets?" Myers asks. He remembers what this is called. "The Purkinje Shift," he tells Lily.

"Sounds like the name of a dance," she says.

He explains how hues deepen in the absence of light. He is excited about his memory coming back. "Don't you see how the colors fade?" he asks.

"Which colors, dear?"

"Never mind," he says.

More and more Lily takes her meals in her apartment. Myers has stopped asking her to let him see it.

In the lounge Myers and Lily sit side-by-side on a sofa and watch *South Pacific* again. He is sick of it. She can't seem to get enough of it. "That's me," she says, "the one on the right with the sarong and bikini top."

"That's not you," he says.

"Pretend it's me. Please." The girl dances in the sand, laughs, and runs into the ocean. A man runs in after her. "That's you," Lily says.

On the screen a chorus of men is singing, "There is nothing like a dame." Myers joins in.

Lily wipes at her eyes. "Oh, dear," she says.

It's the night before Myers is to leave. Vic will pick him up after breakfast tomorrow morning. Myers is eating bacon and fried eggs again. He has gained twelve pounds. He's just managed to fall asleep when he's awakened by the noise of his sliding glass door. Lily stands in the doorway, face pale, the color of the moon. She smells of alcohol.

"Will you come with me?" she says.

"Where?" he asks.

"To celebrate your leaving. We'll steal ice cream from the kitchen. Eat all the peppermint stick we can hold." A breeze ripples her dress.

"It's late. Let me help you back to your apartment."

She pulls away. "No. You must come."

He humors her.

Light from the hallway lights the kitchen. Lily finds a carton of peppermint stick in the freezer. Myers carries it to the counter for her. He opens drawers until he finds a spoon.

"Sit there," she says.

They sit on two metal stools, facing one another. She spoons up ice cream, leans forward, and holds the spoon to his mouth. He inhales the scent of it, enjoys the smooth coldness on his tongue, the bite of frozen peppermint.

"I love you," she says. She takes his right hand and dabs ice cream in his palm.

He pulls back.

"Shh." She moves her mouth to his hand. Her tongue flicks at his palm. He shudders but lets her have her way. "I love you," she says again. "Can we make love?"

"We have to go back," he says. He washes his hands and walks her back to her apartment. They stand on her patio.

Lily inches closer and places a hand at the back of his head. She's wobbly. "Do you want to see the inside of my apartment?"

"Not now," he says.

"Then wait here. Sit there. Don't move. I have a surprise for you."

Myers sits in a canvas chair opposite her glass door. A few minutes pass, then a light comes on behind the drapes. It glows brighter as the drapes open. The garden is washed in white. His skin is white. Her carpet is white. There are three floor-to-ceiling mirrors, a potted palm, track lighting that spotlights garish gold-framed photographs of Lily in various dance costumes, a hula dancer lamp.

The faint sound of music from "South Pacific." Lily appears from the shadows barefoot, wearing a sarong and bikini top. She faces the mirrors and he sees three of her. She moves her hips, almost imperceptibly, an inch to the right, then to the left. Her hands and arms move to suggest ocean waves, a breeze. She faces Myers, takes a few steps toward the sliding door, eyes closed. She stops before she reaches it, drops to one knee, and opens her arms to him.

Myers thinks she has lost her mind, that she is pathetic. But she has been kind to him, a companion during his recovery. Perhaps he should go to her.

A minute passes.

Lily opens her eyes.

She and Myers look at each other. Myers knows what she wants—one last fling, a few moments of pretending she is young again. But she isn't young. She is making a fool of herself, and if he lets her, she'll make one of him. He turns and walks back to his apartment.

Next morning Miss Choy helps him pack and carry his luggage. At the end of the hall she puts his suitcases down and starts to go into the dining room. Myers follows and pauses at the entranceway.

Lily is sitting at their table. She's wearing that wide-brimmed white hat and more gold jewelry than usual. She looks like something imported from the last century. He moves back, certain that she hasn't seen him, and picks up his suitcase.

"You not want to say goodbye?" Miss Choy says.

"Vic should be here any minute," he whispers. "Best not disturb her. I'll wait in the lounge."

# SHARING STARS

We stood facing one another—
caved-in chests, baggy pants,
boxing gloves that reached
past our knees. You're ugly,
Joe said. Shut up, I said, pay
attention and watch my footwork.
Always the teacher, I flicked
three flashing left jabs. Now,
try to hit me. I saw his right
coming, but before I could move,
my jaw wrapped around his glove,
and I was falling forward, floating
through an orange and red and green
galaxy of shooting stars, pleased with
my face, how perfectly it cushioned
my landing. Then I was looking
into Joe's teary eyes. You all right?
Nice shot, I said, then told him
about the stars. Really? he said.
I thought that only happened
in cartoons. He helped me up,
stood before me, and said,
Hit me. Why? I asked. I want to see
the stars, he said. At the time
this made perfect sense. So I hit him.
He lay on my lawn, eyes closed,
a silly smile on his lips. Finally,
he opened one eye and said,
Amazing, friggin' amazing. That
was when I knew how much I loved
him. But he went one way, I another,

and years later, when I heard
he'd drowned trying to rescue
a girlfriend from a rip tide, I felt
as if I'd betrayed him, that I'd failed
to teach him about water and girlfriends.
Then I remembered his wanting to see
my stars. I filled my bathtub,
intending to stay underwater
long enough to know what
he must have felt. I imagined
clinging to a limp body, loving her
so much that I would give my life
to save hers. But my lungs ached,
and without willing it, I sat up
and sucked in air. What I really wanted
was to have him stand still, arms at his sides,
and let me hit him as hard as I could.

# IMMORTALITY

I drove my children
to San Clemente beach.
They were too young
to let run free, too
old to hold my hand.
We stood there, facing
the water, heels sinking
in the sand, the wind howling
its warning, and I told them
how my friend Joe drowned
out there trying to save his first
and only love. I wanted to frighten
them, alert them to the cruelty
in the world. I wondered
aloud what Joe and his fiancée
were thinking as they flailed
and reached out, clinging to one
another for all their love
was worth. And what *was* it worth?
I asked. I saw a look in their eyes,
a weary, bored dullness, and I
understood they had no idea
what I was talking about.
Life, for them, was forever.
I folded my arms and looked out
at happy children screaming
and skirting the waves, and I knew
I couldn't save them. I couldn't
save anyone.

# REFERENCE LIBRARIANS

I imagine them living in dark forests
of knowledge, burrowing in musty sod
and marsh bottoms, sniffing out roots
of ideas, tracing tendrils of thoughts,
separating falacious husks from tasty
nuggets of facts, needing neither fruits
nor flesh, but sustained by the pure air
of curiosity. Easily recognized, they

are shy and preoccupied, often looking
as if they have just come out of a movie
into the light. Most active in the fall,
they always have the winter sniffles
and tend to catch short naps curled inside
cardboard boxes filled with discarded
microfiche. It's common knowledge
they are responsible for those good library
smells and our compulsion to read footnotes.
And consider this: One took six weeks

to translate an obscure Greek palindrome.
Another found the maiden names of all
of Henry VIII's wives in less than a minute.
A third was able to determine John the Scot's
rationale for leaving Charles the Bald and going
to Rome. Think of value received for effort

expended. Consider how little space they take,
their gentleness if not startled, the crimes
and wars in which they have not participated.
You'll find no question too small, no inquiry

insignificant. When approaching them, if their
eyes aren't blinking and they appear frozen
in time, say nothing and walk away. Otherwise,
bow respectfully and ask your question.
Notice how they listen like therapists,
how they take you as seriously as your
mother. One final point: they tend to live
longer than the average person, but when

they die, their souls return to libraries to gently
urge us to lose ourselves in the stacks.
At night when it's quiet, you can hear them
whispering, "Go deeper, go deeper." Open
a book at random and feel them hovering,
inspiring insight, rekindling curiosity
and hunger for knowledge. Follow their call
and you'll leave richer than you came.

# GRAVITY

You're sitting on the edge
of the bed now, naked, applying
lotion to your body, and a tune
is running through my head:
*London Bridge is falling down,*
*falling down, falling down.*
*London Bridge is falling down,*
*My fair lady.*

You roll your pantyhose while
I watch but dare not tell you
that the part I don't get is *My fair lady.*
Is it *her* actual bridge that's falling,
and if so, is she losing it by some travesty?
Or is gravity the culprit here? Could be
her bridge is simply old and tumbling
of its own accord. You stretch the hose

over one leg, then the other and wiggle
into the crotch the way you do,
and, still braless, you turn and ask,
"Aren't you getting ready?"
I'm taken aback by the urgency
in your voice, and suddenly I see
that the falling bridge is a metaphor—
the poet's way of celebrating
the years of pleasure his *fair lady's*
bottom and bodice have given him,
and it occurs to me that gravity
is the expression of the earth's
yearning to reclaim its own flesh. So I say,

"You look fantastic. Come here."
And you do. You fall into my arms.

## POET TAKES OUT TRASH

This morning, while drinking coffee
and reading the paper, I was aware
of your struggle to stuff an orange juice
container into our already full trash. Of course,
I knew I was supposed to leap up and take
it out. But the morning was sweet, the sun's
angle perfect through our window and, still
flush from our outstanding lovemaking,
I was tempted to remind you
of my other talents—the facile way I once
hit a baseball, my show-stopping performance
in third grade as Hansel, the watercolor you like
that I painted of our bathroom. And when you

kicked the bag and cursed, I thought how tolerant
I had been of your faults all these years and how,
even now, I often turn your flaws into poetry.
But I said none of these things, and when
you asked, "Would you please take out the damn
trash!" I took it out without commenting on your
brash afterthought, something to the effect that
you shouldn't have to ask. However, on my way

to that large green container in the alley,
I confess I was composing this poem in my head,
imagining leaving it on the table for you to read,
your wry smile, the small twinge of shame
you might feel at how little you appreciate me.

# AIRPORT REUNION FORTY YEARS LATER

Just walking through this airport
I feel lighter, stronger. And there
you are, at a table, across from a boy
and girl who are kissing and groping.

I'm wild with love. I kiss your cheek
and smell your hair. "You haven't changed
a bit," I say. "You're delusional," you say.
We sip coffee, talk about trips, bad hips,

cataracts, your sister's cancer, my brother's
Alzheimer's. I tell you I take vitamins,
watch my diet, run a mile a day.
There's an awkward silence while we try

not to look at the boy and girl, the hand
that moves under her blouse and into
her jeans. I remember our first kiss,
the heat and humor of our sex. I glance

at my hands, then touch your hair
and ask if you remember how love
felt back then. I want to tell you
I feel it now, but you say you can't

remember what you had for breakfast.
I smile, certain we'll leave this place
together, that by nightfall we'll be outloving
those two kids in the next booth. Your flight

is announced. I rush to tell you
I've been writing poetry and reading

Zorba again. "I really must go," you say,
pulling away. You acquiesce to my hug,

walk a few paces, look back, wave
as if you don't recognize me. I wave too,
and as you pass from view I feel old,
tired. Outside, I spot my bus, board,

knowing I'll never see you again,
that I hadn't seen you this time, regretting
we didn't talk about the important things,
having no idea what those important things

are. I decide I'll stay on this bus and ride
past the airport all day today, remembering.
No, I don't need you, not even my memories
of you. I'll have a ham sandwich for lunch, vote

in November, take a walk, pet the dog
next door, drink Scotch and listen
to Lena Horne. But I don't want to go home.
Not today. At a stop I hear children's voices,

their laughter. I look around and see nothing
but an empty playground with no slide.

## AFRAID OF DEATH

I'm afraid of death—afraid of going
to sleep and missing eternity, of taking
a bite out of some sidewalk
and knowing the instant before I die
that people are stepping over me,
of being the source of the odd odor
coming from my apartment.
I have noticed that people who die
are forgotten. My children will remember
a few stylized acts, their children
a couple of over-told stories, and their children
will know me, if at all, as a hollow
square on their genealogical tree.
I worry about the poetry I want read
at my funeral and who will spread
my ashes. I wonder about the people
who might be present to honor my demise.
No, present is not enough. I want *fully* present
people with sad but enchanted faces. I think
about what I might do to attract more
and sadder people, how I might arrange
to have my memorial video distributed
to those who missed the first show.
I'm concerned about not believing
in an afterlife and stay alert for signs—
a small burning bush, a lost sock
suddenly appearing. I worry
that people who dream up places
like heaven and hell are people
with questionable aesthetics. I don't want
to spend eternity surrounded by bad taste.

What I really want is my friends,
a small room, some books, writing materials,
and a way to make coffee. Come to think
of it, what I really want for all eternity
is something close to what I have now.

# WHAT ABOUT SUSHI?

In the kitchen I'm eating leftover sushi
and listening to Mann and Shank play
tunes from *My Fair Lady* and, like
Professor Higgins, I'm thinking
wouldn't it be nice if everyone
was more like me. There'd be no art
left unappreciated, no cruelty,
no critics, not even a need for grief.

I tap my foot to Mann's driving beat,
take my last bite of Sushi, pungent
with ginger and soy, and I think,
what about Sushi? I love eating it
but have no interest in making it.
I'll keep a few sushi masters around
for special occasions. And while I'm at it,
we'll need more buttery Julia Childs
to get through the century. Shank delivers

a soaring climax to "The Rain in Spain,"
and I decide we'll need more Shanks
and Manns, too. More Bachs and Vivaldis,
a Beckett or two to nudge us in the side
and ask us why we're waiting and just
what we intend to do. Mann pounds
his bass, crashes his cymbals, and ends
with an ascending sweep of celestial
chimes. The air smells like the sea,

and I imagine a great tapestry of life
held together by the marrow of every

living thing, extending from the first
cell forever forward to the unknowable
future. And here, on this spot, I eat
the last grains of rice, grateful for sushi
and for everyone and everything I'm not.

## SEASON TICKETS

Fifteen years we've had them,
the two seats at the end of Row 29,
Section 20. We were real fanatics
back then, screaming, high-fiving,
thinking this would last forever.
We hardly noticed when,
seven seats down, a woman
in her sixties, a city-league
tennis player, stopped coming.
Turned out she'd had a stroke
and died. Next season the woman's
husband had a heart attack. During March
Madness the person five seats down—
an irrepressible man with a white
beard and a Greek fisherman's cap
who called himself Uncle Charlie—
died of throat cancer. *Treatable*
was the last word we heard him say.
Next season Uncle Charlie's nephew,
a despondent accountant who
quoted Rush Limbaugh, disappeared
one day. Died from cancer, we heard
from his wife who sold their tickets
to a woman who was killed jaywalking.
Her seat was empty the entire season
but filled with waiting. JoAn is next
in line, then me. The team is younger
this season, less experienced, losing more
than winning. JoAn and I watch
with greater discernment, nod and clap
instead of scream, take deep breaths

between baskets, and look forward
to time outs. An obese adolescent
sits in the seat next to JoAn now.
He eats hot dogs and yells *Go Cats*
at odd times. We both wish him well and hope
he lives a full and happy life, but it's apparent
he knows nothing about the game.

## WHAT I DIDN'T SAY
*(for JoAn)*


As a man who stays inside a lot
I'm always surprised when spring
comes and your flower garden
is suddenly alive, how we become softer,
laugh more, wear brighter colors.

This morning from the kitchen
window I watched you work
the soil, the light that shone through
olive leaves and formed delicate
shadows on your face. I closed
my eyes and, for some reason, thought
of our deaths—mine and yours—how
this life we've patched together,
these flowers, and even this tremulous
fear will die with us. You swept

the patio, pinched off a few dead
leaves, and came inside. I must have
looked at you funny because
you smiled and asked, "What?"
"Nothing," I said, but that wasn't true.
You see, what I wanted to say,
the exact thing I wanted to say
and didn't, was Thank you.

## AT THE ANNUAL FRIENDS
## OF THE LIBRARY SALE
*(for Raymond Carver)*


I found a hard cover copy of *A New Path
to the Waterfall,* marked with a big yellow *R,*
his last book, poems written when his feet
had gone numb and his lungs were covered
with tumors too numerous to count.

I opened it to the last page and felt
his presence, the faint scent of leather
and tobacco, the lapping of water
against a bow, the lazy flap of a
sail, his voice, barely audible,
nothing left but a whisper.

I owned a copy already, but bought
this one anyway. It cost a dollar and
when the woman who took my money
kidded me about being a big spender,
I asked if she had ever heard of Raymond Carver.
She said she didn't believe she had,
so I opened the book to the last page.
Listen to this, I said:

*And did you get what
you wanted from this life, even so?
I did.
And what did you want?
To call myself beloved, to feel myself
beloved on the earth.*

That's lovely, she said. Is he still living?
Oh, yes, I said. More than most.

# *acknowledgments*

---

My deepest gratitude to Nancy Wall for her unflinching support, instruction, and endless hours of proofing; to Meg Files for nudging me to the edge of the abyss and urging me to jump; to Barrie Ryan for her gentle encouragement when the ego was most fragile; to Tom Speer for his quiet persistence and easy grace; to Leila Joiner for her talented eyes and ears and her sense of humor; to Andrew Cozine for his wit, his penchant for the bizarre, and gallons of strong coffee; to Masha Hamilton for infectious strength and honesty; to Bernadette Steele for her support and generous reads; to Steve Hanson for the one insight no one else had. In loving memory of Deborah Gately-McKeen and Joe Hofmaister.

"Sharing Stars" and "Immortality" are for Joe Hofmaister. "Airport Reunion Forty Years Later" is for Jane Thompson.

"Okies" and "Seabreeze" were each awarded first prize for prose in successive issues of *SandScript*. "Okies" placed second in the annual Raymond Carver Fiction Contest.

# *about the author*

Dan Gilmore, in his time, has been a white trash Okie, a fry cook, a student, a draft dodger, a soldier, a draft counselor, a jazz musician, a starving actor, a minister at a Reno wedding chapel, a graduate student, a psychologist, a man divorced as many times as he has married, a single parent, a college professor teaching statistics, physiological psychology and aesthetics, a college dean, a consultant to business, and, more recently, a full-time writer trying to make sense out of an essentially random but full life.

# other publications
# by Pima Press

*My Father's Shoes*, Tom Speer

*Woodpiles*, Robert Longoni

*How the World is Given to Us*, Barrie Ryan

*The Swiftness of Crows*, Nancy Wall

*Tandem Space: Daughter-Father Poems*, Carmen Speer, Tom Speer

Orders, inquiries and correspondence should be addressed to:

Pima Press
c/o Meg Files, Chair
Department of English
Pima Community College West Campus
2202 West Anklam Road
Tucson AZ 85709-0170